Just in Rhyme

UNDER THE SEA

by Toni McKay–Lawton

Illustrated by Eddie Manning

Rans♦m

a crab is quite a crusty chap
with two big pinchy claws
he scurries sideways along the
beach
and loves the sandy shores

dolphins frolic in the waves
and swim the open sea
they glide and dance the
                    day away
happy to be free

a shark has lots of great big teeth
a pointy tail and fins
he swims along very quietly
but be careful when he grins

seahorses are quite small it's
                              true
with very curly tails
it helps them cling on tight
                    you see
when the ocean beds they
                       trail

a whale is just enormous
with a mouth that's very wide
he's really very beautiful
through vast oceans he can
glide